W. E Brown

Jack and Jill

A Love story

W. E Brown

Jack and Jill
A Love story

ISBN/EAN: 9783337327941

Printed in Europe, USA, Canada, Australia, Japan

Cover: Foto ©Andreas Hilbeck / pixelio.de

More available books at **www.hansebooks.com**

JACK AND JILL

A LOVE STORY

By W. E. BROWN

Illustrated by Elisabeth Curtis

PUBLISHED FOR THE BENEFIT OF

THE SILVER STREET KINDERGARTEN SOCIETY

OF SAN FRANCISCO, CALIFORNIA

WILLIAM DOXEY
San Francisco

CONTENTS

CONTENTS.

LIST OF DRAWINGS.

11

PUCK TO LYSANDER.

On the ground sleep sound;
I'll apply to your eye,
Gentle lover, remedy.
When thou wakest, thou takest
True delight in the sight
Of thy former lady's eye;
And the country proverb known,
That every man should take his own,
In your waking shall be shown:

    Jack shall have Jill.

    Naught shall go ill.

SHAKESPEARE.

Midsummer Night's Dream, Act 3, Scene 2.

EPIGRAM.

When Jill complaines to Jack for want of meate,

Jack kisses Jill, and bids her freely eate;

Jill sayes, of what? sayes Jack, on that sweet
　　kisse,

Which full of Nectar and Ambrosia is.

The food of Poets; so I thought, sayes Jill,

That makes them looke so lanke, so ghost
　　like still.

HERRICK'S HESPERIDES.　1648.

DEDICATION

To Kate Douglas Wiggin, the pioneer in free Kindergarten work on the Pacific Coast, this volume is inscribed, as a slight token of regard for her unquestioned genius as an instructor, and her charming aptitude as an author. The free Kindergarten class, gathered through her efforts, on Silver Street, San Francisco, September 1, 1878, was the first school of its kind established west of the Rocky Mountains. This modest undertaking, enlivened at first by the sweet chatter of less than twenty little ones, was the initial attempt that has culminated in that meritorious group of Kindergarten schools on this Coast, that now counts its teachers by hundreds and its pupils by thousands.

PREFATORY

'

Of the sixty-five millions of people, living in these United States, it may be asserted, without risk of contradiction, that more than ten millions have, at some period of their lives, been familiar with Mother Goose's story of Jack and Jill. No metrical romance could be more simple in construction or versification,—no incident could be more briefly narrated, for the edification of infant minds.

In other countries and at other periods, a single line or verse of a ballad, arranged in rhythmic iteration, has moved multitudes to deeds of daring, and sometimes to acts of violence. During the reign of terror in France, millions of men and women were urged on to cruel and malicious persecutions by the wild refrain:

"Ah! ah! ça ira, ça ira."

The evolution of this popular song has a romantic and tragic interest. "Le Carillon National," the air to which the words were sung, was a favorite composition with the Queen of France, and the music room of the Palace of Versailles, presided over by Gluck, was, in her happier days, filled with the strains of this captivating melody, often accompanied on the harpsichord by the Queen herself. A few years later, by the awful irony of fate, the hideous hurdle that bore Marie Antoinette to the guillotine was surrounded by a tumultuous crowd of men and women, singing to the tune she had loved so well the terrific words:

"Ah! ah! ça ira, ça ira!
A bas, les aristocrats."

A hundred years earlier, all the cities of England were ringing with a melody that assumed the startling proportions of a national song:

"Lero, lero, lilli burlero,
Lero, lero, bullen a-la."

Senseless as the words appear they were set to a catching air that was whistled, played, or

sung, by half the population of the kingdom.
Macaulay says of it: " From one end of England
to the other all classes were constantly singing
this idle rhyme," and in Boswell's Life of John-
son, Beauclerk is represented as saying: " The
ballad of Lilliburlero was once in the mouths of
all the people of this country, and is said to
have had a great effect in bringing about the
revolution," (of 1688).

But the time-worn quatrain of Jack and Jill
has a simpler significance and a more peaceful
mission. From Shakespeare's time to the pres-
ent day, this familiar conjunction of names
has been used to represent the exponents, in
rustic life, of the sweet affluence of early love, as

21

Darby and Joan represent the matured affection and loving attributes of a happy married life, supplemented by an old age of fireside comforts and genial surroundings. It is to be hoped that this literary venture will not be the means of removing the amiable personality of Jack and Jill from the entrancing realm of ideality to the more commonplace sphere of individual experience. There is no intention to dispel an illusion so fascinating by an agency so unpretending.

It is a consummation much to be desired, that the sweet fairy tales of Perrault and the Countess d'Aulnoy, the Melodies of Mother Goose, the absorbing story of Santa Claus, the historic wonders of William Tell's heroism, and all nar-

ratives of a kindred class, may escape the vandal
touch of iconoclastic meddlers ; that recitals
like these, dedicated to childhood's dreamful life,
may forever remain among the cherished remin-
iscences of that story-telling and story-listening
era, which all look back upon as a season of
unalloyed delight. It may be urged by some
that our subject is too simple to be thoughtfully
considered; but when it is well known that a
distinguished German naturalist wrote two pon-
derous volumes upon the growth, beauty and
vitality of the wings of a butterfly, it will not be
thought a trivial matter to devote an idle hour
to the distinctive characteristics of Jack and Jill.

INTRODUCTION

On the 31st of August, in the year 1688, a notable event occurred in connection with the literary history of England. On that day, John Bunyan, the author of Pilgrim's Progress, died in the city of London.

During the same month of the same year, there was born in the city of Boston, in the State of Massachusetts, Elizabeth Vertigoose, whose parents subsequently changed their name to Vergoose, and finally abbreviated it to Goose. This infant girl, born into the world at about the same time that Bunyan left it, became the author of a little volume, published in 1719, called "Songs for the Nursery, or Mother Goose's Melodies for Children."

It will not be thought inappropriate to consider the lives and productions of these two authors, as having similar characteristics and similar results. Both were born in poverty and of obscure parentage, and the daily avocations and personal surroundings of both were simple, primitive and uninviting. With an education limited to the merest rudiments of English study, they both produced, in a widely different sphere, literary work that found a more enormous circulation and a more varied class of readers than any other secular writings of ancient or modern times.

Both of them lived in an era of puritanic severity, of wide-spread superstition, and of barbaric persecution. Both were early imbued with strict orthodox principles, and strange as it may seem, their literary success and their literary fame were found in the alluring realm of allegory. With the sad experience, the unjust persecution, and the embittered life of Bunyan all the world is familiar; but of the uneventful career of the other personage mentioned little is known. In the office of the City Registrar of Boston we find recorded, under date of June 8, 1715, the marriage, by the Rev. Cotton Mather, of Elizabeth Goose, Spinster, to Thomas Fleet, Printer. Elizabeth was then twenty-six

33

years of age, and her husband was twenty-eight. He came to Boston at the age of twenty-one and started a printing house, doing most of the work himself upon a hand press; and it was upon this hand press that was worked the first edition of Mother Goose's Melodies. If a veritable copy of this first edition could now be found, with its first page illustrated by a long-necked goose, the bibliomaniacs of to-day would emulate each other in bidding for its possession.

After the wedding Mr. and Mrs. Fleet took up their residence with the bride's mother, Mrs. Goose, who was at that time a widow living in Pudding Lane, now called Devonshire Street.

In 1720 a son was born to the expectant house of Fleet, who was in due time christened John. Jack, as he was called in the home circle, was a charming boy, and the maternal instincts of the grandmother were stirred to their loving depths by this sweet scion of her race.

Here we have an ideal home of a mechanic of the colonial period: The stalwart father and bread-winner, working at his trade; the mother, busy with household cares; and the grandmother, watching with gentle assiduity the sweet inmate of the nursery. Three generations of loving hearts, beating with sympathetic throbs, and culminating in the glad fruition of paternal, maternal and grand-maternal joys; each happy in the performance of cherished and genial duties, and each feeling that the air of their humble home is made musical by the gentle cooing of the infant boy. As the months go by, Jack becomes the life and pride of the family circle. His special pet, however, is his grandmother, to whose sole care he is most frequently consigned; to her loving lips he gives his sweetest kisses, and to her listening ears his earliest words. His gentle presence and personal contact bring new comfort into her life, and sweep away the growing cares of age.

The opportunities for reading and study in those days, for families like this, were exceedingly rare. Mrs. Fleet had none of the advantages of a library to stimulate her mental powers. With the exception of her Bible and Pilgrim's Progress, the books she loved the best and read the most were Bishop Burnett's History of the Reformation, Baxter's Call to the Unconverted, Fox's Book of Martyrs, and Milton's Paradise Lost. In view of an experience so circumscribed, it would seem to be a striking evidence of the intellectual elasticity of Elizabeth Fleet's brain, that it could withstand the sombre and depressing influences of literature like this. In the composition of all these works the form of imagery prevailed, and the genius of allegory controlled the evolution and elucidation of the narrative. It is not strange, therefore, that this young mother should have imbibed the same spirit in the construction of her melodies.

In these later days, when her songs of the nursery are sweetly intoned by the mother's gentle voice, the infant ear catches the rhythm and the infant mind treasures up the affluent flow of words. But the adult reader sees a deeper meaning in the grotesque lines, and oftentimes takes great pleasure in the attempted solution of these jingling couplets, so fraught with weird and quaint superstitions.

In 1723, when Jack Fleet was three years old, the busy housekeeper, inspired by the

38

crooning lullabies of grandmother Goose, pre-
pared and published a second edition of her
melodies, and dedicated the volume to her
little son. This new publication contained
several versified narratives not found in the
first edition. Notable among these were Jack
Sprat, Jack Horner, Jack the Giant Killer,
Jack and the Bean Stalk, The House that Jack
Built, and Jack and Jill: the latter taking
rank among the sweetest and choicest of our
author's allegorical work. It does not need
the cipher and cryptogram of an Ignatius
Donnelly to fathom the charming love sketch
that lies hidden in these four lines:

Jack and Jill went up the hill,

To get a pail of water;

Jack fell down and broke his crown,

And Jill came tumbling after.

Jack and Jill are two ideal lovers,—too young to love wisely, but not too young to love well. The hill mentioned in the verse represents the difficult love problem they are determined to solve; their going up simply means an honest desire to overcome all obstacles that an unsympathizing world may put in their way. The empty pail, that they carry between them, symbolizes a life without love,—an existence without hope; and the sweet anticipation of reaching the summit, and filling the pail, re-

veals to them the joys that are in store upon
the culmination of their ardent desires. Jack
and Jill, though young in years, are inspired
by the instincts of older heads. They sen-
sibly determine to restrain the rapture of their
youthful hearts for a brief period, until the
serious realities of life shall assume a rosier
hue. But when each feels the throbbing pulse
and the warm hand-clasp of the other, on
their journey up the hill, their wise resolves
are scattered to the winds; Jack, no longer
able to control the loving impulses of his
heart, "falls down," and Jill, in genial and
sympathetic mood; comes tumbling after.

Were it possible for the spirit of the author

of the original Jack and Jill to revisit the city of her birth, and she were called upon to rewrite the story of these two rustic lovers, she would, perhaps, with the experiences of the nineteenth century before her, and the culture of her native city all about her, throw allegory aside, and give a new version of her familiar story.

JACK AND JILL

A LOVE STORY

IN AQUARELLES

I.

JACK and Jill went up the hill,

    With empty water pail they started;

No thought of accident or ill,—

    Jack full of fun, and Jill light-hearted.

II.

They left their cozy little home,

    Their kitchen fire as yet unlighted;

Thus in the crispy air to roam,

    Each satisfied, and each delighted.

III.

THEY could not make a cup of tea,

    Nor coffee boil, not even a little;

Where'er they turned, they'd always see

    An empty pail or empty kettle.

IV.

But yet these lovers knew no thirst,

    Dreaded no future, as they ought-ter,

Although 'twas obvious from the first,

    Their cottage was devoid of water.

V.

HEY hunted high—they hunted low—
  No instant did their efforts stop;
Jack said " There's none;" Jill said " That's so,
  There isn't a drop—there isn't a drop."

VI.

Jack sweetly smiled and said to Jill,
  In accents soft that never fail—
" I know a spring far up the hill,
  Let's go there, darling, with our pail."

VII.

HIS tender glance, his thoughtful words,
  Touched the sweet sense of gentle Jill,
As oft the mellow song of birds,
  Will bring to lovers' hearts a thrill.

VIII

Jill wants a holiday, and sees
  The very thing she wants, in sight;
A day with Jack among the trees,
  A picnic full of rare delight.

IX.

HE hastens to an inner room,
    And hurries on a dress of chintz;
Fair fabric from a Lyons loom,
    A symphony in floral tints.

X.

She gathers up her soft brown hair,
    A shining, glimmering, rippling screen;
And with it trims her forehead fair,
    With a low fringe of golden sheen.

XI.

HE then puts on her broad straw hat,

And ties it round her dimpled chin;

And Jack's warm heart goes pit-a-pat,

To see Jill's smiling face within.

XII.

She grasps her flowing skirts with care,

And lifts them with a modest grace,

'Till her fair ankles gleaming there,

Bring rosy flushes to her face.

XIII.

SHE steps upon the bending grass,
　　Light-footed as a bounding fawn;
The loveliest, gentlest, fairest lass,
　　That ever trod an emerald lawn.

XIV.

Her bonny face is lit with smiles,
　　Her blue eyes sparkle in the sun;
Her laughing words and artless wiles,
　　By Jack are treasured one by one.

XV.

Her winning ways are all so rare

   He lays his rapture at her feet;

She seems so gracious and so fair

   So sweetly pure—so purely sweet.

XVI.

Jack takes the hand she offers him,

   A hand ungloved, and soft, and warm;

He presses it with earnest vim,

   And gazes on that lovely form.

XVII.

E put his arm around her waist,

And p... on ... ...

Something to ... ...

An... now ... ...

III

Jill ... ...

And Ja... ... to ... ...

With ... the ... ...

... he ... ...

XIX.

OW turn they from their cottage door,
   Beneath those radiant summer skies ;
Of mutual love an endless store,
   Reflected in each other's eyes.

XX.

Thus, hand in hand, this loving pair,
   On culinary thoughts intent,
Pushed out into the morning air,
   And jointly braved that steep ascent.

XXI.

P toward the summit of the hill,
  Each holding by the empty pail,
They climbed and paused—and climbed, until
  Their home was hidden in the vale.

XXII.

Anon, they rested in the shade,
  And watched, with ever-glad surprise,
The flashing beauties of the glade—
  The gilded wings of butterflies.

XXIII.

HEY heard the murmur of the bees,

And the soft low of distant herds,

That fed beneath the sheltering trees —

Alive with flashing, twittering birds.

XXIV.

Jill, light of foot, flew on apace,

Thinking she first might reach the water;

But Jack, impatient, made the race,

And, eyes all bright and smiling, caught her.

XXV.

" Don't hurry so," said honest Jack,

 " In sunshine or in cloudy weather,

We'll neither falter nor turn back,

 But fill our water-pails together."

XXVI.

Jill's eyes replied, and it would seem,

 They spoke a volume as they gazed,

So soft their hue, so bright their gleam,

 As to his face her look she raised.

XXVII.

THEY gathered blossoms by the way,
  And listened to the wood dove's call;
Jack frank and happy   blithe and gay
  Jill daintiest blossom of them all.

XXVIII.

The skies grew brighter as they walked,
  The earth seemed fairer where they ranged;
And as they wandered there and talked,
  The very landscape's tints were changed.

XXIX.

THEY found new joys in every place —
    The grassy fields seemed lovely parks;
And floating down etherial space,
    They heard the notes of unseen larks.

XXX.

The hedge rows glistened bright with dews —
    Wild flowers were jewels in their eyes —
A panoply' of crimson hues,
    And purple shades, and yellow dyes.

XXXI.

HE bright drops, from the lingering haze,
    Seemed only glittering for them —
Grouping themselves on fairy sprays,
    And every spray a diadem.

XXXII.

Along the brook, through bending ferns,
    They saw the sunlight's fluttering beam;
And heard, among its curves and turns,
    The murmur of the rippling stream.

XXXIII.

By the sweet waters' soothing flow,
   They gently rest on mossy seats,
And words of love in accents low,
   Are whispered in those calm retreats.

XXXIV.

And now they reach the crystal pool,
   And now they see reflected there,
Upon that mirror, smooth and cool,
   Their radiant faces, bright and fair.

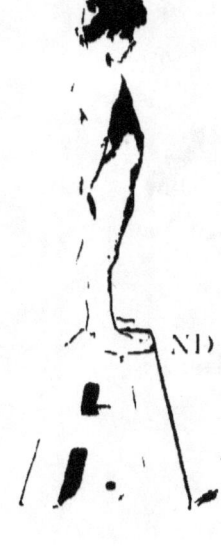

XXXV.

AND as they linger near the shore,

Upon its clear, unruffled tide,

The sunlight paints in sweet relief,

Their shadows nestling side by side.

XXXVI.

Each loving glance, from each, invites

A gentler phase of life's young dream,

And every happy movement writes

Its sweet caresses on the stream.

XXXVII.

HE hours seem minutes as they fly—
　The waning day declines too fast;
And every hour that passes by,
　Is all too beautiful to last.

XXXVIII.

Meanwhile, " Our empty pail is here,"
　Said smiling Jack to smiling Jill ;
" Let's fill it to the brim, my dear,
　And then we'll hasten down the hill."

XXXIX.

O sooner said than it was done,

    Jill's heart was true, when Jack besought her;

And when her sweet consent was won,

    The water-pail was full of water.

ADDENDA

JACK AND JILL

AS IT MIGHT HAVE BEEN WRITTEN

BY THE AUTHOR OF

"LADY CLARA VERE DE VERE"

———

Honest Jack and pretty Jill,
  From me you shall not win a word,
About your journey up the hill—
  I merely hint at what occurred.
You crossed the lawn, at early dawn,
  And lingered slowly as you went,
To gather daisies on your way—
  To sniff the wild flowers' earliest scent.

Pretty Jill and honest Jack,
    A lowlier poet must rehearse,
How you went up the hill and back,
    Then tell your story all in verse.
With empty pail you left the vale,
    Each bound to each by playful oath,
That you would brave that rugged hill—
    And love lent eagerness to both.

Honest Jack and pretty Jill,
    Your loving hearts are full of mirth;
The sweetest annals but fulfil
    The simple story of your birth.
If some should fear, as you appear,
    While on your, *upward* march you went,
That you might falter on your way,
    Others would smile at your *descent*.

Pretty Jill and honest Jack,
  Why did you climb that hill at all?
Why venture on that dubious track,
  And risk your chances for a fall?
Water is found on lower ground,
  In springs that gush and streams that flow;
Far better then to stay near home,
  And take life easy as you go.

Honest Jack and pretty Jill,
  I see you in your garden seats,
Where graceful lilies lift their heads,
  And fragrant roses pour their sweets.
No millionaire, that breathes the air,
  Can ever boast such happy hours,
As you enjoy from day to day,
  Within your gates among your flowers.

Then, pretty Jill and honest Jack,
    There seems no reason for your climb,
Along that upward path and back—
    It was a very waste of time;
With such a wealth of rustic health,
    You should be happier far than they,
Who close the doors of lovely homes,
    And wander all the live-long day.

                                        W. E. B.

JACK AND JILL

AS IT MIGHT HAVE BEEN WRITTEN

BY THE AUTHOR OF

" My soul to-day
Is far away,
Sailing the Vesuvian Bay."

———

Jack and Jill

Went up the hill,

Their empty water-pail to fill;

The morning sun

Had just begun

To kiss the dew drops one by one.

Jack's spirits rise

In glad surprise,

To see the smile in Jill's blue eyes.

They seem to him,

Full to the brim,

With lights that gleam, and shades that swim.

Jill loves to go

Where zephyrs blow—

And when the early golden glow

Touches her rare

And soft' brown hair,

Jack sees a lovelier radiance there.

In dreams, by boat,

They skim and float,

From scenes near home to scenes remote;

In happier dreams,

They seem to roam,

From scenes remote to scenes near home.

They love to climb,

And pass the time,

On simple slopes or hills sublime;

And lowing cows,

Neath drooping boughs,

Their childhood memories will arouse.

Their thoughts are told
In words of gold—
They each to each their hopes unfold.
At work or play,
Throughout the day,
Their cares and griefs are put away.

Where'er they meet,
In lane or street,
Their lives are lovely, pure and sweet;
Each hour of light—
Each day and night
A very billow of delight.

When sunset pours,

Through open doors,

Its purple tints and golden stores;

They bid good-byes

To sunset skies,

And chant their evening lullabies.

W. E. B.

JACK AND JILL.

AS IT MIGHT HAVE BEEN WRITTEN

BY THE AUTHOR OF

" One morn a Peri at the gate
Of Eden stood, disconsolate."

———

One morn his dearie, at the gate
Of Jack's rose-garden, stood elate ;
Watching with clear and tranquil eyes,
   The early dawn's imperial flushes,
Spreading along the eastern skies,
   The first of bright Aurora's blushes.
Each ray but added to the grace
And beauty of that rustic face.

'Twas an enchanting scene and fair,
To see Jill and her lover there—
Counting the minutes, one by one,
Ere they should greet the rising sun.
An empty water-pail is swinging
    Between the two, as thus they stay—
Both smiling sweet, and sweetly singing,
    Their anthems to the coming day.
They have a hill to climb, and so,
Their thoughts go upward with the glow.

The rosy dawn comes on apace,
And morning perfumes fill the place;
As sturdy Jack and lovely Jill
Commence their journey up the hill.
They watch the sun, now rising higher,
    Without a care—with no heart troubles—

Except that on their kitchen fire,

   No sparkling water boils and bubbles.

And so it is, this happy pair —

   This nature's son and nature's daughter —

A rugged steep thus jointly dare,

   To fill their empty pail with water.

And now the purling springs they seek,

With lips that smile and smiles that speak;

And thus it comes —when eyes meet eyes,

With questions mute, and mute replies,

They find that each is giving each,

A thrilling language without speech.

Their life is one' of happy rest,

With youth their lot, and love their guest.

In gentle mood, they loiter long,
With here and there a burst of song;
The slow receding landscape seems
Like pictures painted in their dreams;
No chilling or disturbing breeze,
Rustles the foliage of the trees;
The shadows linger cool and still,
While radiant sunbeams kiss the hill;
And Jack sees every brilliant hue
Reflected in Jill's eyes of blue.

And thus they wander to and fro,
Laughing and singing as they go;
Their every impulse fresh and fair,
Their voices filling all the air.

Like those gray cooing birds, whose throats
 Send from afar, whene'er they meet,
Their tremulous and tender notes,
 So soft, so plaintive and so sweet;
That pure love language of the birds,
Expressed in warblings, not in words.

With such blithe accents, Jack and Jill
Sing to each other on the hill.

W. E. B.

JACK AND JILL.

AS IT MIGHT HAVE BEEN WRITTEN BY

WALT WHITMAN

———

I celebrate the personality of Jack!

I love his dirty hands, his tangled hair, his
  locomotion blundering.

Each wart upon his hands I sing.

Pæans I chant to his hulking shoulder-blades.

Also Jill!

Her I celebrate!

I, Walt, of unbridled thought and tongue,

Whoop her up!

What's the matter with Jill?

Oh, she's all right!

Who's all right?

Jill.

Her golden hair, her sunstruck face, her hard
and reddened hands;

So, too, her feet, hefty, shambling.

I see them in the evening, when the sun em-
purples the horizon, and through the dark-
ening forest aisles are heard the sounds of
myriad creatures of the night.

I see them climb the steep ascent in quest of
water for their mother.

Oh, speaking of her, I could celebrate the old
lady if I had time.

She is simply immense!

But Jack and Jill are walking up the hill.

(I didn't mean that rhyme.)

I must watch them.

I love to watch their walk,

And wonder as I watch;

He stoop-shouldered, clumsy, hide-bound

Yet lusty,

Bearing his share of the 1-lb. bucket as tho' it
    were a paper-weight.

She, erect standing, her head uplifting,

Holding, but bearing not the bucket.

They have reached the spring.

They have filled the bucket.

Have you heard the "The Old Oaken Bucket?"

I mourn the downfall of my Jack and Jill.

I see them hill descending, obstacles not heed-
ing.

I see them pitching headlong, the water from
the pail out-pouring, a noise from leathern
lungs out-belching.

The shadows of the night descend on Jack re-
cumbent, bellowing, his pate with gore be-
smeared.

I love his cowardice because it is an attribute,
just like Job's patience or Solomon's wis-
dom, and I love attributes.

Whoop!!!

CHARLES BATTELL LOOMIS,
In N. Y. Independent.

JACK AND JILL.

AS IT MIGHT HAVE BEEN WRITTEN BY

AUSTIN DOBSON.

———

Their pail they did fill,
 In a crystalline springlet,
Brave Jack and fair Jill,
Their pail they did fill,
At the top of the hill,
 Then she gave him a ringlet.
Their pail they did fill
 In a crystalline springlet.

✳

They stumbled and fell,
 And poor Jack broke his forehead.
Oh, how he did yell!
They stumbled and fell,
And went down pell-mell.
 By Jove! it was horrid.
They stumbled and fell,
 And poor Jack broke his forehead.

CHARLES BATTELL LOOMIS,
In N. Y. Independent.

JACK AND JILL

AS IT MIGHT HAVE BEEN WRITTEN BY

ALGERNON SWINBURNE.

———

The shuddering sheet of rain athwart the trees!
The crashing kiss of lightning on the seas!
  The moan of the moist night-wind on the wold,
That erstwhile was a gentle, murmuring breeze!
On such a night as this went Jill and Jack,
With strong and sturdy strides, through dampness black,
  To find the hill's high top and water cold,
Then toiling through the town to bear it back.

The water drawn, they rest awhile. Sweet sips
Of nectar then for Jack from Jill's red lips,
    And then, with arms entwined, they homeward go;
Till mid the mad mud's moistened mush Jack slips.
Sweet heaven, draw a veil on his sad plight,
His crazed cries and cranium cracked; the fright
    Of gentle Jill, her wretchedness and wo!
Kind Phœbus, drive thy steeds and end this night!

CHARLES BATTELL LOOMIS.

In N. Y. Independent.

JACK AND JILL

AS TOM HOOD WROTE IT

IN TWO LANGUAGES.

Jackus et Jilla, ille et illa,
  Fetchere aquam, went up the hill.
Sed cecidit Jackus, cui caput est crackus,
  Et Jilla, et situla, met with a spill.

TOM HOOD'S ALMANAC, 1842

www.ingramcontent.com/pod-product-compliance
Lightning Source LLC
Chambersburg PA
CBHW032151010726
47493CB00008BA/2652